OP HERRICK 12

IN MY OWN WORDS

To order additional copies of this book, contact:
Xlibris
UK TFN: 0800 0148620 (Toll Free inside the UK)
UK Local: 02036 956328 (+44 20 3695 6328 from outside the
UK)
www.xlibrispublishing.co.uk
Orders@ Xlibrispublishing.co.uk

ISBN: 978-1-6641-1365-7 (sc)
ISBN: 978-1-6641-1366-4 (e)

Print information available on the last page

Rev. date: 12/29/2020

"I have to start by thanking my awesome wife, Rebecca. For being the best mother and wife anyone could ask for. She was a rock on the day she dropped me off at the camp gates, having the knowledge that this could be the last time we could see each other if the worst was to happen. This woman is the strongest person I have ever known.

Secondly, the next person I would like to thank is my uncle Jeff (who has been like a father figure to me throughout my life).This man has always been there if I've ever needed someone to talk to and he showed this massively on my return. (Stop thinking about that pink elephant...)

And finally, Carol (my mother). I have put this woman through a lot growing up, I will never forget leaving for Scotland and seeing the look on her face of how proud she looked that I was finally sorting my life out .That look got me through a few dark days in Afghanistan."

This is my thoughts and feelings on what happened on Herrick 12 in Afghanistan. A seven month tour in Uppervalley Garesh in Helmond Provence and a short stay in Molvern.

Sunday 28th March

I left home at 21:00 hrs with my wife Rebecca and Evie-May to head to camp Marne barracks to get on the transport to go to Afghanistan for a 7 month tour.

I got to camp about 21:15 hrs and said my goodbyes, it's hard to put into words the heartache and the pain I felt on the short journey to camp. When I arrived at camp I looked in Evie-Mays eyes and thought to myself that this could be the last time I would see her little innocent face and that broke my heart, the pain I felt at that time was like my heart had just cracked in two and that's when the tears started to come, after I gave Evie-May my goodbye kiss I turned to Becky and just looked in her eyes and said i'll always love you and I will see you soon I promise. That's when I gave her the biggest kiss and a long hug. Whilst I was hugging her I was trying to take in everything the smell of her hair, perfume and weirdly how she looked, I just didn't want to forget her beautiful face and smile not for one second, because I didn't know if I was going to see her again and that hurt!

When I got out of the car I headed towards the transport and I said to myself (you will see them again, I promised myself that) then I turned around and waved for the final time.

Sunday 28th March 23:00

I got on the coach and set off to the airport Brize Norton, Rebecca had given me an envelope to open on the coach. When I opened it there was a picture of Evie-May, Becky and I and a letter saying how much she loved me and a card off Evie-May with her big girl writing. This just started me of again.

The coach trip took so long to get to Brize Norton well it felt like it did!

Monday 29th March 03:30

After a five hour coach journey we eventually arrived at the airport and checked in, for once it went smoothly and that's a change for "1 MERCIAN". After all the bags and weapons were checked in I gave Becky a phone call and then gave my mum a call.

That was a hard call to do because I knew that she was proud off me for doing what I was doing but I knew that I was her little boy still and it was breaking her heart me going but if I didn't join the army I would be dead or back in prison for a long time.

<u>08:45</u>

So after all of the goodbyes we boarded the plane and headed to Cyprus for 24hrs. We arrived there at 13:00 to refuel the plane. Whilst the plane was getting sorted I gave Becky a quick call to see how she was. I didn't think she would be in bed she finds it hard to sleep for a few days when I go away especially when I'm of to "HELL".

<u>Tuesday 30th March 05:00</u>

So we arrived in Afghanistan (Camp Bastion). It was a bit of a whirlwind to start but once the "head sheds" sorted there shit out it calmed down and we got our accommodation (tents) and settled in for a few day ready for R.S.O. I package (Reception, Staging, Onward Movement, and Integration).

<u>12:00</u>

We started the "R.S.O.I" with briefs the briefs were about the layout of the ground we were going to and how the Taliban were laying there I.E.D's (Improvised Explosive Device) because they are always trying to change their tactics to kill us. After that we had a quick look at the "FOB'S" (Forward Operating Base) in Helmond and what had changed in the past 24 hours in the "green zone".

<u>Wednesday 31st March 06:00</u>

After a terrible night's sleep I got up and headed off to the ranges for day 2 of the R.S.O.I. We started with the usual H&S (Health and Safety) and hygiene brief (death by power point), and then went on to an E.C.M (Electronic Countermeasure) brief that took us up to lunch. Many of the lads pay "lip service" to these briefs but this equipment will keep you bloody alive. It's always the inexperienced lads that don't get it.

After lunch we started to zero our weapons on the ranges and find out any problems which we might have. We finish about 17:00 and headed back to the tents and to get some "scoff" (tea).

<u>Thursday 1st April 05:00</u>

Day 3 of R.S.O.I, this is the start of the acclimatisation which was (2.4km) tab this is to get your body used to the heat of the country. We got to the pickup point and boarded the battle bus it reminded me of the movie good morning Vietnam what a bag of shite. We got to the ranges at 07:00 and started the day's briefs on R.O.E, (Roles of Engagements)

C.A.B.C, "medical refresher" and on the med chain (MERT, PEDRO CAPABILITYS etc), influence and psyops.

13:00 after lunch we started with C.Q.M ranges (T.L.F.T.T), stop & search, detention & detain handling then finally we finished with evidence collection & exploitation (Inc x-spray and biometrics). Finally after a long hard day we headed back to camp for tea.

Friday 2<u>nd</u> April

Day 4, we started at 07:30 for G.P.M.G refresher (General Purpose Machine Gun) "fam shoot" after the faming we went to the E.C.M practical man pack (very heavy)! The look on the new lads faces were a picture, this was the first time that they have ever put the man pack on and I knew what they were thinking ha, ha, ha (been there done that). After that we went to the environmental health speech which took us up to lunch.

13:00 fob defence live firing "B.E" Inc med skills and casevac practical assessments. It opened my eyes how bad some people were at some drills its easy when you're in the uk and its not for real but as soon as you get to war lads start to flap "what the fuck have I got myself into working with these"

16:00 the start of coin trg. Insurgents and why they fight defeating the insurgency then we moved on to M.A.O.T, Heli ops. After that the G4 chain brought us our tea (range poo). Disgusting, the one thing that you want after long day training is a nice dinner but they can't even do that WOW!

19:00 fob defence at night this wasn't that bad actually I think because they had a bit of training in the day they blew some cobwebs off. The interpreter came who uses charter com which the Taliban uses to communicate in the field and it was alright. That brought us to 22:30 and we went back to camp. Out of the 4 days that was the best.

Saturday 3<u>rd</u> April

Day 5 we moved out at 09:00 to start T.E.W.T- operating in complex environments and working with the population. After that we commenced to ground sign awareness practical (op BARMA). Pain in the the arse but a life saving drill. After that we went to the dismounted patrolling skills B.E (multiples). This incorporated the following (ground sign, vp identification, I.E.D confirmation, mark&avoid, contact I.E.D, casevac, H.L.S drills, working with the interpreters). This brought us to the last stage of the day theatre realities and mission rehearsals.

Sunday 4<u>th</u> April

Day six we started at 05.30 for another long day of everything we had learnt over the past few days on R.S.O.I.

After all the assessments were carried out the battalion had the go-ahead to commence in Helmand. So we went back to the tents and started to pack up our kit because we were moving out the next day this is when is sort of sunk in that tomorrow I could get my first kill.

Saturday 10th April

A few days has past now and were still in Camp Bastion. We got told that we were moving out on the 5th but it got delayed don't know why.

Well I got woken up this morning to "OP wide awake" my first thoughts was "Longy" that he had been hit because he got told that he had 20 mins to get his stuff ready and he was deploying with the Danish Army to "Camp Prise" for a few month, this was last night and were still waiting to find out if it was or wasn't his call sign that got hit.

I've been working with the colour bloke today sorting out the ammo which was left over from the last lot. What a fuck about it was no wonder the army is in shit state the amount of stuff which the Scott guards got rid of because of damage and we have just found tons of ammo and equipment just dumped (joke)!

I thought it was a good idea to take my top of whilst I was sorting out the iso yeah bad idea, i'm burnt from head to toe (I hate being an undercover ginger).

11th April

Not done much to day I went to sort out the rest of the iso and then went to watch some TV "C.S.I". I can't wait for later I'm going to phone Becky I've not spoke to her in days. Just got back from scoff and op minimize was on so I can't speak to Becky and Evie-May it's hard not to get pissed off because you know the only reason that it gets put on op minimize is because a call sign has been and someone has been hurt, I suppose you just have to deal with it, these things happen.

At 15.00 we heard an explosion about 2 km away so that's probably what it's for, let's hope everything is ok.

We've got a few more days left here and that's when the games start can't wait. I just want to get out there now it going to be crazy for the next six month and I hope I come back with all off my limbs. I've got my R&R date (Rest and Recuperation) now so I'm not home until 26th July so that's something to look forward to.

22:55 One more day over. For the past three hours I've been sorting out 9 platoon two section's lads out with their kit for some reason the head sheds have put most of the new lads all together and it just doesn't work you need some experience in a section. It makes you think if they can't admin themselves in camp what are they going to be like in the "fob Sanford" and most importantly what are they going to be like in contact. I don't know how half of them passed out of training well we'll soon find out when were in the green zone.

12th April 21:51

Just got back from the C.Q.M.S (Company Quartermaster Sergeant) and were half way though sorting out the kit to take with us. All the kit we have is at least 12 years old and the stuff that the previous regiment had left us is diabolical parts missing of stuff bits broken and stuff that we were meant to have we don't. I don't know who did the hand over take over but whoever has they need a kick up the arse. I got told that the Danish Army is helping us out with the move to the fob that's going to be interesting! They had seven iso's to move and three on the route have been blown up already. "So what does that say for our move out". There's quite a few lads flapping at the minute about the move I don't blame them my arse is twitching a bit.

The mail came today and the phones came back on to can't wait to speak to Becky later. I got two parcels and six letters it's like buses you only want one but six come at once, ha, ha, ha. Two were of my mum and four were of Becky and Evie-May. It was nice just to read a nice letter and forget about where I was for a few minutes.

13th April 22:39

"What a day to day has been," I got woken up about 4 ish with two loud explosions and dust hitting my face and heavy gun fire shortly after with small arms and then a couple of jets passing by. I don't know exactly what happened but I think that the Taliban tried to blow.

Once again I've been working with the C.Q.M.S trying to sort out all the stuff we need for the fob, trying to get tent poles around here is like asking the Taliban for a day off. It's shocking that we need to hunt for equipment days before we deploy.

It's been a hot day today nearly in the 40's my face feels like a crisp packet and my arms were still burnt from the other day.

The section commanders came back this afternoon from Sanford after being on a ground recce (Reconnaissance) for the 16th. The fobs aren't that bad as first thought. They have been built up more than we have anticipated the engineers have been busy in the past few days. They said we have a bit of work still to do when we get there but not as much as previously thought.

On there recci they were told that the locals aren't happy at the moment because "ISAF" (International Security Assistance Force) opened up on a coach full of civvies and killed 30/40 and injured a hand full. So we will have our hands full when we get there, it's safe to say that their pissed off! I have got a brief soon so I should find out more info about it.

THE MOVE OUT

<u>20th April</u>

We moved out to the fob four days ago, i've not had a chance to write for a few day's because it's been too hectic so I'll start with the journey to the fob.

We moved to the heli pad in the middle of the night to go to the fob. On the way our chopper was shot at and they started to do defensive monovers for the rest of the way. I wouldn't mind but I hate flying and I was asleep when the flares fired out of the side of the shnuck. Then you just heard the rounds hitting the belly and the sides and the RPG's (Rocket Propelled Grenade) flying past that's why the flares on the schnook were deployed fair to say I shit my pants. That was the first time I thought about dying and I hadn't even had a chance to get a foot on the green zone yet.

When we eventually got to the fob I was gobsmacked at the state of the place it was inhabitable, i'm not joking. There was stagnant water everywhere the accommodation (Tents) had rips in them and the burns pit was just a foot deep. It took three days to sort out, we basically stripped the camp and rebuilt it.

11

My call sign "fox trot 42" and "fox trot 43" went out on our first foot patrol to the local school, the construction workers got shot at last night so we got told to go and find out what happened.

So our c/s's (Call Sign) went out towards the green zone to talk to the village people whilst c/s f43 went to the school. On route we found our first IED it was 150 m out of camp, whilst we were sorting out the IED c/s 43 got ambushed on the edge of the green zone.

They got one casualty a gunshot to the leg. We also got two kills on with a UGL (Under slung Grenade Launcher) and the other with small arms. Whilst this was going on the thoughts were horrible rounds flying past your head people screaming, shouting and just the disorganized flapping of section commanders. This is just because it was their first contact and you're bound to flap a bit "I know I did".

We got back into camp about two ish and the O'C (Operational commander) was waiting to speak to us about what happened and an update on our casualty. He was ok just a scrape!

After the O'C spoke to us about what had happened (Pep Talk) he broke the news that at 17:00 we were going out again guess where? To the same place were c/s 43 just got ambushed to show them we're not afraid and more important not defeated. "I wouldn't mind if he was coming with us"! I'll write some more when I get back (lets hope ha, ha, ha).

22:00 well yeah got shot at (Shook). What a nightmare fighting at night in the dark. It's hard enough in the day trying to keep control of the platoon in a fire fight let alone in the dark. We were skirting the green zone and then all of a sudden hell broke out rounds slapping at my feet and flying past my ears it got that close some times that I felt the vortex of the round my god that was close. But I've got to give it to the section we fucking gave it to them.

23rd April 14:27

Well a few days have passed now it's a bit too much to write every day your just patroling, eating, cleaning your weapon and if you can sleep, that's when you're not getting woken up by mortars.

So where do I start? On the 21st we got our orders for an op that we were going on that day.

We moved out of camp early doors about 06:00 to move into compound 34 in Rehimkai for the next nine days to start dominating the ground and taking it back of the Taliban.

The kit was unbelievable just imagine I had my GPMG, water, food, bits of clothes "i.e." socks and foot powder (Nice) for nine days, the weight was so heavy it must of weighed at least 100kg and we had a 5km tab to do with possible fighting on the way.

The patrol to compound 34 was ok no contacts it was an easy tab to it.

On the 22nd we were established in the compound that's when the fun started, I'm so glad that it started when I dropped my kit.

It was about 14:00 when c/s 42A and 42B went out on a routine patrol from the compound. The patrol was approximately 200m. They left the compound and headed down me axis though an alleyway and turned left that's when they got ambushed with an IED, they were only 30-50m away from me. All of a sudden a massive explosion went off, the force of it knocked me on my arse and them shooting at the Taliban, and I knew straight away that we would have casualties. The day had just started to get shit!

I got myself up with ringing in my ears and started to try and locate the Taliban it was hard because of all the dust and my eyes were burning with all of the shit that got thrown up in the explosion.

42 started to extract back to the compound when the Taliban ran around to cut the c/s off and started to throw hand grenades over the wall. We found out later that the IED was a command pull so at least the ECM is working.

When they extracted back to our location they had three casualties Pte Warring 9 platoon, Pte Scot (TA) and Lance Corporal Mc Carfay also 9 platoon.

Pte Warring's injures were facial he was the front valum man he took the main impact of the blast. His teeth and his top lip was gone there was blood everywhere he was just saying "find my teeth" I think that was the morphine talking.

Pte Scot had nails though his right hand and all up his arm and a piece of frag hanging of his ear.

L/CPL Mc Carfay had shrapnel all up his groin and legs. After the initial casivac we got the Danish Army to come and pick them up and got them to a (HLS) for Pedro pick up. They were 100m to our rear flattening poppy fields for the police station to go later that year. At this time Pte Crichlow was on the roof with me and shouting" he saw a man about 80-100m away next to a wall".

I told him to engage and drop the dirty bastard. That's when he got a stoppage. He was shouting that he couldn't run over to him that's when I saw the Taliban pointing a long barrel weapon at him. He didn't have a clue that he was just about to get a round in the back of his head.

I threw my jimpi towards him and his face was a picture and then just jumped at him. I landed on top of him and he said what the fuck are you doing and I said you owe me I'll explain later.

I picked up my jimpi and located the enemy and started to fire. There were round's slapping the wall what I was leaning on and dust going every were Crichlow was shouting "that's it Si kill them, fucking kill them."

After a few more bursts I shouted to him get your fucking minimi sorted i'm nearly out you fuck-wit. He just looked at me and at that point we just started to laugh.

The feeling at that time was a feeling i've never had. I was mad thinking back I was getting shot at rounds flying past my head and I was just laughing my head off at the situation we were in.

After we killed four of the Taliban and it all calmed down we were observing our arks for more enemy, that's when I saw one male popping up and down in the area that we just had the fire fight in. I had him in my sites and I asked my platoon sgt if the R.O.E (Rules of Engagement) had changed and he said "no if there's a threat engage because we have 422 & 421 out on the ground" which meant you can open up at dickers and IED teams. I was following him for a few seconds and I saw a phone so I shot him straight in the face. That was a strange feeling to shoot someone whilst looking straight at them. One minute he was alive and the second minute his head cracked open like a melon and his lifeless body just dropped to the floor with a puddle of blood around him.

422 & 421 went to the contact point and to try and get some info on what the Taliban are planning next. That's when the c/s went to the dicker and reported that he was a dicker and approximately 10 to 15 years old and asked what they should do with him.

COMPOUND 34

23rd April 2010

Not much sleep last night, allsorts going through my head from yesterday about the I.E.D and the kid I shot. I just kept thinking could I have done anything different, I know it's stupid but it's playing on my mind.

I don't mind killing grown men but young kids is a different story. I don't mean I like killing men it's just easier if that makes sense.

It was about 10:20am when I saw a motorbike on stage on the roof that's when I noticed a motorbike was going up a dirt track and dropping of people, the bike must of dropped 4 people off I felt that something just wasn't right so I paid most of my attention to that area for a bit.

I got my binos out and started to look up and down the track for any tell-tail sings of an I.E.D team that's when I saw a line of rocks just set off the track which was telling the locals that they were planting an I.E.D

I called over my Plt Sgt to confirm what I was thinking and he agreed with me. He called on the net for any call signs in the area and a call sign told him that they were about to approach that grid. We then got the go ahead to shoot to kill because off the immediate threat of life.

I adjusted my site and got in position and waited for them to pop up.

It was about 600/700m away after about 5 minutes they came into site and I opened up on them after 150 round's I stopped and asked for eye star to fly over the area and inform back to me if the diggers were down.

Eye star confirmed four bodies were down and one was dragging himself away to the north. They said that he would probably die later due to his injuries. After that at 14:00 we moved out back to the fob to carry out our rotations (patrols, guard and q.r.f).

25th April 2010

We went on to Q.R.F that night when we got back, 43 c/s were pinned down by a sniper so we got stood to. After a while our sniper and my c/s got our orders to flank the Taliban sniper. Also to engage so our c/s that was pinned down could move and get back because they were low on ammo.

We got in position and started to engage their sniper after a while the Taliban's firing stopped, our sniper got a head shot and the rest started to run back in their hole's where they belong.

We moved back to camp and met up with the c/s who we gave fire support to. Both c/s started to shake hands, hug and started to laugh at each other. The camaraderie around camp was electric.

26th April 2010

We got are orders today for an op(Objective Lock-it) to give support to the engineers whilst they built a foot bridge and a vehicle bridge.

We were going to get split into two c/s one was going to give support to the engineers and the other c/s was a supply/Q.R.F team (Quick Reaction Force). This was a shit task, back and to all day taking water and batteries to the c/s out on the ground.

18:50

Just got back from drop off for the CSM who are in compound 30 (Mud Hut). We got given two vehicle's (Mastiff) doing the re-supplies on foot was just not working the area that the c/s were in was 3km away. After all day up and down to them, all of the lads were shattered, so very kindly they gave us some vehicles!

The patrol out was good and the drop of went smoothly. On the way back we were passing two buildings and that's when a brick hit my arm and just missed my face. There was only one route in and out so it was quite easy for the locals to do stuff like this. Thinking back it could have been a grenade.

That's why you don't use the same roots all the time. It gives patterns to the enemy.

All the c/s is starting to close back in from the green zone soon, so my c/s is going back out to give support on the ground. Once that it's done we have a night off to sleep. In the past five days I've had about twelve to fifteen hours sleep so I'll be sleeping like a baby. That's if we don't get mortared.

28th April 2010

We moved out at 04:30 to continue with objective "Lock It" our c/s was switched around so now we're main support.

We moved down to the river and entered the green zone. After we got into place we heard that icom charter had picked up that the Taliban were going to assault us by the north. At this time we thought they might because the atmospherics were changing with the locals. It's a tell-tail sign that something was going to happen. The Taliban tells them to move out so they can attack.

Ten minutes later the icom said that they were in position and ready to engage us.

We got our Q.B.O'S (Quick Battle Orders) to fix bayonets because where we were going to flank we couldn't see more than a foot in front because of the long growth of the field. We got told to push down in the valley and go into an extended line and push East.

We started to push East when icom said that they could hear something in the field. We got told to holt and stand by to engage. After about 2 minutes which felt like 2 hours the Taliban opened up on c/s 41, it sounded like that they had a lot of fire power. My section commander shouted to me to push right on my own and engage them so they could push forward and clear the enemy position.

So I picked up my GPMG and legged it around the section that's when my section commander said to me be careful you're on your own. We both nodded and I left to get into position.

When I was in position I opened up on them and then the rest of the section attacked the enemy and killed all of them.

After our c/s cleared the position then realized that there was another enemy punker.

We called up to c/s 41 to start engaging the other position. That's when they told us over the p.r.r's (Personal Role Radio) to get down stand by for shake and bake!

After it all settled down we did a search patrol to the enemy position, "what a site" it was the first time i've seen a shake and bake basically a shake and bake is, the shake part is a U.G.L and the bake is foss i.e. blow them up and then burn them. (affective but not a nice site), body parts everywhere and the smell of burning flesh.

After we cleared the area we pulled back and moved back to camp.

29th April 2010

We got orders last night at 22:00 for today's mission. We got told that we were going to head back out to the green zone (North) and left flank to Taliban and push them (West).

We moved out before first light 04:30 to cross to bridge which the engineers built the other day.

We got there on time and crossed over the bridge into the green zone.

After we crossed over we gave the company fire support whilst they crossed over.

We moved East down the river bed and found a possible I.E.D so we backed up and marked and avoided it and found a new route to the East.

At this time the rest of the company was getting into position when icom chatter picked up that the Taliban could see troops in the river and field.

The other half of our platoon was in the river bed and we were in the field.

The icom chatter said that the Taliban were going to start shooting in five minutes when they were ready. Just as we heard that one of the lads went down with heat illness so they dragged him back to the supporting platoon.

After he got casie-vaked we got pinned down by a sniper from the North it was coming from compound 1-3. Everyone was jumping for cover, round's were hitting at your feet. (That's one contact that you don't want to be in) you just don't know where it's coming from and your just waiting to get hit.

My view was covered by trees and most of the sections was to thank god.

After a few minutes the A&A (Afghan army) moved to high ground to get a better look of the area.

We then started to get mortared by them so the A&A started to engage them. We called for fast air for support due to our lack off mobility on the ground, this took about thirty minutes and then the jets flew over and dropped H.E (High Explosive) on the mortar team and that was that.

It's a strange feeling being out here. Three hours ago I nearly got shot and now I'm sat in a jackal writing this and it's happening on a day to day basis. I just hope when I go on R&R my head isn't too messed up. You do get use to getting shot at and shooting people how do you then go from that to standing in a queue at Tesco 48 hours later?

30th April 2010

Not much has happened today still on Q.R.F and only been out once for a re-supply to c/s 42A's compound. And then the rest of the day just did some admin. After lunch I phoned home and spoke to Becky, not much has changed everyone is fine.

Just before I heard some lads talking at the back of the tent's about writing a poem so we came up with this. It's about the other day when we got pinned down by a sniper. I thought it rounded everything up about what has happened over the last few days.

THE DAY OF THE SNIPER

Carrying a stretcher and sweat in my eyes, we came to a wall and a sudden cry.

The wall collapsed upon the man, we were in the stream but it felt like a dam.

I'm against a wall and hear gun fire, then hit the ground and begin to cower.

The boss shouts sniper and we hit the deck, but were trying to see and shot his neck, we're confused and can't see where, when 30 mil shoots through the air.

It kills the sniper and we all cheer as it's one less reason for us to be here.

1st May 2010

Got crashed out this morning on Q.R.F. C/S 43 we're getting twated in the green zone. They were getting contacted from the front and the rear with R.P.G'S and I.E.D'S they called fast air in to fly over. We got no casualties and the call sign killed five Taliban.

Its frustrating being on Q.R.F, it's just a waiting game when you're on it, all you want to do is to get out there fight and help your mates out.

2<u>nd</u> <u>May 2016 17:15</u>

I got up today at 03:45 to leave the gates for 04:30 for our next mission called (Op Smash 2).

We left the gates for 04:30 to head towards compound 11 then into the green zone.

We reached the compound and dropped off our snipers for overhead cover and then continued North where call sing 34 got ambushed the other day.

After dropping of the snipers we got about 300 meters when we got ambushed. There was about ten to fifteen Taliban in two different locations, after a short fire fight we withdrew back to a compound that Tac took over that day. They were 50m South of us.

Just before we got to the compound we got flanked by three pax with small arms and R.P.G'S.

All of a sudden we just heard the whistle of the R.P.G and it landed next to Huffy's feet and he just took to the air and landed ten feet away, after a short while and with a few lads shouting him he just got up and looked around then said "fuck me how have I still got my legs". We all dropped to the floor and started to fight the Taliban. We got a signal that the Taliban was in a mud hut in front of us so I got called forward to give cover fire whilst all the c/s could get to Tac's location.

I ran to a ditch in front of everyone and shouted for a link man. After a short time I knew no one was going to come so I quickly linked up a few rounds and started to shoot at the house. No one had any smoke grenades left so I used my rounds for that effect. I started to fire left and then right after about 100 rounds hitting the walls the dust was getting thicker and it was working.

I shouted to the c/s to move back so they moved to Tacs compound. After all of them were in they gave me some cover so I could move.

Once we were in the compound the Taliban tried to take over they were hitting us from three sides. We all just mounted the wall and started firing "it was like off a western movie", this contact lasted for about 2 hours not a long one compared to some fire fights we have.

After it all calmed down we then bugged out to sniper house to re-group. The route we took was a different one and it was through a sewage(it was barfing) the smell was deadfall. Once we got through the sewage we re-grouped in the sniper house and I went straight to the roof and opened up on the Taliban.

Whilst we re-grouped, they did and then they started to fire at us. R.P.G'S once again flying past our heads and one of them hit the top of the wall I was firing from. The blast of the explosion knocked me back and I fell off the wall. All what I can remember is waking up to a big head in my face shouting something but I couldn't hear because of the R.P.G. I checked myself out and then got back up on the wall and I was just about to fire when I noticed that my barrel was bent a bit, so I changed it and then started to fire at them.

I started to think my days were numbered for a bit because this fire fight was lasting for quite a bit and I was running out of ammo. A short time later they started to withdraw and the fight was over. I was left with 150 rounds and a fucked barrel.

We started to withdraw back to the fob and re-group. After getting back we found out how many casualties we had. We occurred four casualties cat C to B non life threatening and we killed about twenty five Taliban so not a bad day for the army.

19:00 Just got some mail from Becky it's about time not had any for a while can't wait to read it.

3rd May

10:27 Just been told that Cpl Holmes and Cpl White has been injured in Sangin by a R.P.G Cpl Homes has died due to his injuries and Cpl White is a Cat A. It just hits home when something like this happens and how real it is and how close I've been to getting hit a number of times.

God rest Cpl Homes soul we will always think of you. And get well soon Whity.

14:00

Just got back from a patrol. We patrolled to the towns school, when we were half way to the school we got told from our interpreter that icom had picked up that the Taliban could see us and if we head in to the green zone that they were ready to fight.

We needed to go to the edge of it because last night the South Sanger saw some activity in a field. They thought that two pax was digging in an I.E.D or that's what they think anyway.

So we needed to check that out then go to the school. Even with the icom charter we headed towards the river just on the edge of the green zone. We started to do a route clearance when we got told to collapse and head back to camp and not to go to the school.

When we got back we got a brief of the boss about the patrol that we were on. He told us that 30-40 Taliban was heading south towards us and icon was picking bits up. Then we got told that the village that we were going to patrol through the Taliban laid an I.E.D two hours before so that's why we got told to come back in it was too much of a high threat.

6th May 20:37

Just got off Q.R.F and guard I've been on it for the past few days.

Yesterday I spoke to Becky and Evie-May which was a long time coming. The past few weeks has been hard physically and mentally. On the 4th PB'1(Patrol Base) got attacked by mortars and small arms and homemade grenade's. The Danish army were in there when they attacked and they took a lot of casualties 9 cat one's and three cat two's.

The Taliban assaulted them when a sand storm hit. The Danish casualties were missing legs, toes, fingers and a few had frag to their head. Let's hope there ok. That must have been unbelievable to go through that.

10 platoon went yesterday to bump their numbers up so they can secure the camp. They weren't happy about going but you just need to go when you're told that's the nature of the beast in this job.

<u>22:04</u>

Just got off orders for the op were on tomorrow. (NOT GOOD) a local came to camp today and told us that the Taliban had laid I.E.D'S in Rahim's town. (The same place we were blown up last time). So we have to go with ATO and help them clear the area for the locals.

The OC gave him a tin of spray paint and asked him to spray were they are and where the command pulls are.

To me this is a bit risky to trust a local because you can't trust them not one bit. Let's hope I can tell you tomorrow if he's screwed us over or not!

This might be my last thing I will write so, I love you with all of my heart and soul Becky and Evie-May and I will always .x.x.x.

<u>12th May 2010 19:19</u>

"So where do I start". I'm alive anyway. So in the last few days i've been shot at every day more lads have been blown up and i've got no credit to phone home and it's to bloody hot. As you can tell i'm having one of them days.

On the 8th Jones 81 got shot in the leg on stag in compound 34. We told the boss that it was to dodgey because we needed to come out of the compound and go into the Sanger and the back of the Sanger was wide open to the green zone. What a joke!

The Taliban was so sneaky. One of them had an orange dish-dash and walked past the Sanger to catch the attention of the Sanger when the other twat pre dug a murder hole in a wall he shot him from behind. He got shot in the back and the back of his legs.

<u>10th May</u>

We got told that the Taliban had laid more I.E.D'S in Rahim and the informer had pre marked them. So we moved out early doors and cleared the route into Rahim. Before we got to the marked I.E.D'S we found some more which was (low metal content) that took all day and my first thoughts were we got set up. If the informer new about the other I.E.D'S why didn't he know about these ones?

<u>11th May</u>

We deployed into the green zone for a shura. This was to meet the village elders to try and get them on side.

When we stopped and went into all round defence we got told off icom chatter that the Taliban were setting an ambush up for the c/s they could see and that was my call sign.

We were only about ten yards from their killing zone when we got told to stop and go firm and pull back. When we got told what they were doing over the net we quickly extracted out of there. That was a close shave!

Once we got back on the track were we left the other c/s that was doing the shura we formed back up and headed back to camp.

On the way back the Taliban moved out of their ambush and started to open up on us from the rear. After a few bursts we R.T.R'ed and extracted back into camp.

<u>14th May 10:10</u>

I've been on Q.R.F for the past few days, not much has happened. Last night c/s 41 found an I.E.D in wood line just behind the police station. A.T.O flew in this morning to dispose of it.

Spoke to Becky the other day, I needed to hear her voice. The phone call went so quickly. You need to watch how long your on it, it doesn't last long. I need to wait till Monday to speak to her now, no more cred left.

<u>17th May 21:48</u>

The last few days I've only done a few G.D.A patrols nowt really happened. But today is a different story!

We got are orders last night to go to Kandak a village which is anti ISAF to try and flush out the Taliban and it worked.

We were meant to leave at 04:00 but a storm came last night so it got pushed back to 10:00. We left and went in to the green zone and it's going good no icom chatter and the atmospherics seemed ok. After pushing 300m into to green zone it all kicked off.

We moved to compound 2 and then the icom picked up that when we move out of the compound there going to start shooting at us. So we got our fire support ready on the high ground and then we moved out. We had targeted to a stream with round's hitting the floor "I don't know how we didn't get shot".

So we pushed left flank and the A&A were meant to push them back but it didn't quite go to plan. The A&A just pushed forwards 100m and stayed there (bunch of twats).

So that's when we got the go ahead to fix bayonets and advance to contact, "What a rush"

We pushed forwards and came under contact and killed all 6 of the Taliban, with round's, U.G.L's and grenade's.

Whilst this was happening the A&A had two casualties. That made a lull in the battle for a bit until mert came for them.

After they got picked up we advanced forward and pushed the Taliban back to the East, somehow the Taliban had reinforcements and then they pinned us down for a bit by a P.K.M.

After a short fire fight we pushed forwards and ran over there firing point and cleared it. There were bodies everywhere, it got annihilated with U.G.L'S, fos, grenades, 5.56, and 7.62. It was like a movie from world war 2.

Once we took over the area from the Taliban we started to move back to camp. We headed to compound 9 as a rally point. When we reached the compound we got put in reserve section because we had just been in the main fire fight. I went straight to the roof and then saw a dark dish-dash running across the field with a long barrel weapon, I aimed my gympee and got a stoppage. I shouted to the rest of the company which was heading back to camp to look right and to engage but by this time he had gone into dead ground.

I got my orders to collapse my position and to head out of the compound to move back to camp. After a few minutes on the track we started to come under fire (single shots) this must have been the man I saw on the roof.

The first shot just missed the man next to me, we all went to ground for a moment to try and locate the shooter.

No one could truly locate the sniper so we got told to hard target back to camp. Whilst we were zig zagging back to camp rounds kept getting fired one at a time. I think it was the fifth round that got fired when I felt the vortex of the round go past my head. It must have only been one to two inches from my head. I fell to the floor and just looked over my arm and saw everyone just running for their lives back into camp. So I got myself up a ran as fast as I could. All what I was thinking was if they shoot me no one could drag me into camp because I was the last man and there not chopping my head off on the internet.

Once we got into camp I just dropped to the floor, I just couldn't breathe, I was running for my life.

After we unloaded our weapons we all started to laugh about the day and tell each other our war stories over a brew

Over all not a bad day. I've been shot at, pinned down by a sniper and nearly died. "All in a day's work for the infantry".

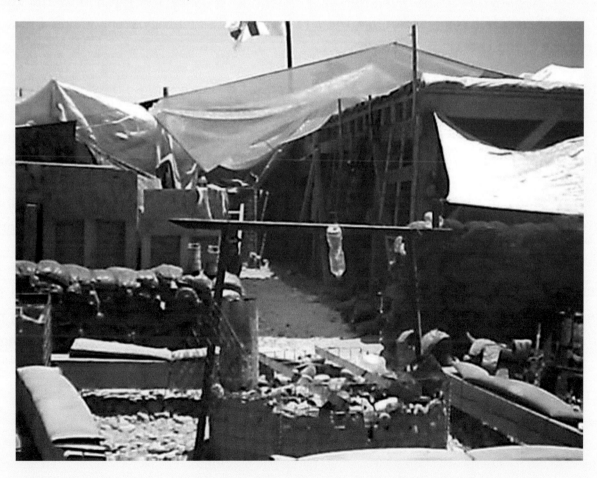

26th May 12:58

I've been in Malvern (PB) for a bit now. We took over a Danish c/s because they had been getting hammered a fair bit in the past month. They've had five casualties and need rest bite for a while.

We were there for about six days without any incidents and then it began.

The first explosion hit 42c, there call sign was patrolling down a foot path to the West of the PB. The track was only 5-6 meters away from the front gate.

42c c/s was 15m down the track when they saw some ground sign, so they decided to mark and avoid and skirt around it. When half of the call sign went past the Taliban detonated the device and L/Cpl Green got hit by some frag in his left hand. They then fell back into the PB and the medic started first aid on him.

About forty minutes after the explosion our boss gave us some Q.B.O's to go out and to try and locate the firing point. So we got ready and headed out.

We headed North about 50m and then went West into a field. We past an irrigation ditch and went into another field. The two front valon men were at the top end of the field and then the section commander told them to go firm. Just as they stopped an I.E.D was detonated in the corner of the field.

After I picked myself up and dusted off my face that's when I saw Goldie and Cindy were hit. Goldie the section commander was screaming "my arm my fucking arm". I started to run up the line and take control of the incident and told the section to give us all round defence. After the initial shock of the explosion the section started to work together.

I told two lads to sort Goldie out and call Jones over to me. I knew Cindy was in shit state. I got to him and he was gasping for air so I ripped off his off spray and there was blood everywhere, they must have been ten holes in his chest.

I shouted over for as many first aid kits that I could get my hands on and started to plug his holes. Whilst I was sorting out Cindy I kept looking over at Goldie trying to find out his condition so I could call for a casi vack. Whilst all of this was going on I had the platoon commander on the net to me asking me "what was going on and who was the casualties and the state of them".

After a short time "which felt like an hour" I made the decision to move the casualties back to the field in front of the PB so the chopper could pick them up and the medic could come and give me a hand with Cindy because we were losing him.

I told the two lads to get Goldie up and move him to the field in front of the PB and don't forget his weapon. Then the rest of the section would give me rear cover and side cover. The last thing that I needed was to get contacted again.

I told Jones to get his stretcher out and we were going to move Cindy. He got it out and then we moved him to the field where the platoons medic was there waiting and sorting out Goldie. After a short time they came and picked them up.

Cindy had a punctured lung, broken ribs, broken collar bone and frag to his neck, hand and arm.

Goldie had a broken left arm and frag up his left side of his body.

That was the worst day so far because they were two of my closest friends and I thought Cindy was going to die!

28th May 2010

It was a normal day and my moral was picked up a bit because it was Evie-May's Birthday. After I spoke to her and Becky I left on a patrol.

We pushed out and went towards the same irrigation ditch where we got blown up the day before. The two valum men pushed over the ditch and Cpl Tonner the new section commander was about to step over to ditch when the I.E.D detonated. From where I was truly thought that we had a K.I.A on our hands.

After the dust settled the only people who were injured were Tonner and Millican. Tonner had shrapnel to his bicep and Millican had it up his legs.

After we called in the mert we extracted back into the PB and the boss got told to start trimming us because of what's been going on the past few days. It was needed, since we have been here we have had five casualties and seen a lot of action in the green zone and on the wall's.

2nd June 2010

It was such a hot day no cold water and not much shade.

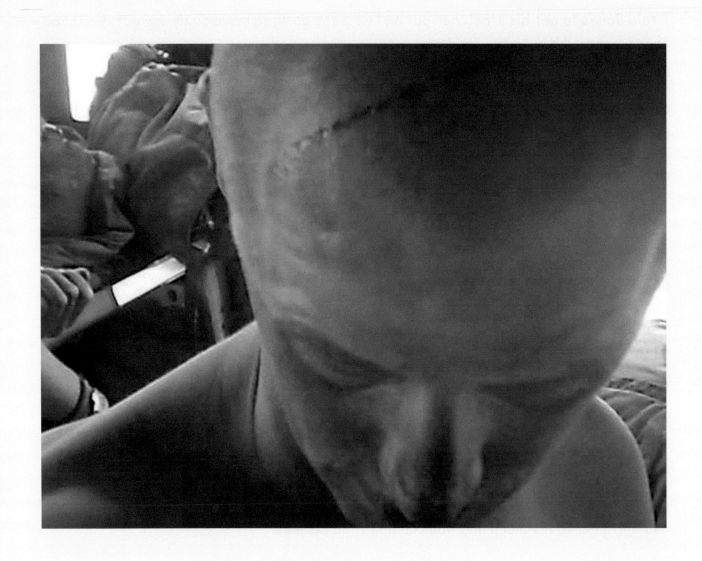

We decided to play a bit of poker on our down time because we were only doing stag, the patrols had been stopped for a few days which was a nice change.

We were playing for a while when all of a sudden the PB started to come under fire R.P.G's were flying over and hitting the walls.

It was the strangest thing because one second we were playing poker and then the Taliban was trying to kill us. I can just remember the look on the lads faces when the R.P.G hit we all just shouted "yes come on lets go".

I ran a grabbed my G.P.M.G and mounted the wall and started to fire back.

That's when I saw the amount of Taliban they were. They literally were 360 around us. The amount of fire power was inmence, there was every weapon firing at the same time. My ears were ringing it was so deafening. After a fair bit I can just remember my head flicking back and then I must have blacked out. I woke up on the floor and my head was burning so bad and that's when I knew I had got shot in the head luckily just skimmed me. I don't think you can get closer than that!

5th June 2010

6 platoon came to the PB to replace us and the next day we took them out for a G.D.A of the ground. We were out for about one hour when we got contacted from the East. It wasn't a big contact so we cracked on with the patrol. After we had shown them the main firing point we moved back to camp.

The next day 6 Plt went on a patrol on their own and whilst they were out they got into a fire fight. We all got stood to and mounted the walls so we could give them some fire support for their extraction back into camp. Whilst they were moving back we saw dickers on bikes and they were on mobile phones. So we got the go ahead to kill them. It was a "turkey shoot", lads just laughing and shooting at the Taliban. That's when I thought some of these lad's have seen too much and there messed up. Five Taliban died that day.

14:00

It's so hot today I'm getting sick of this heat and I just want some cold water, all what we have is bottles of water which have been left in the sun all day. I would kill for a nice ice loll right now!

6th June

Six and part of nine platoon went out on a patrol to the H.L.S today. Half way down the field of the H.L.S there was a donkey staked down. We didn't think much of it because it's been around for a while. Until one of the front lads from nine platoon noticed a fishing wire coming off it and heading to the wood line. They pulled back and told 40a (CO) over the net what that they have seen but he just laughed and told them to carry on.

The next day we went out on a patrol and avoided the donkey and crossed over a track which was called i.e.d. road. Which is meant to have over 29 i.e.d's on it.

When we were heading back we skirted past the donkey and that's when it blow up. No one was hurt they put the shrapnel on the wrong side and it all went away from us.

Our boss sent a contact report up to the OC and told him that it was a donkey I.E.D and that shut him up.

The next day we were meant to have been leaving for Rahim but the Taliban flooded the field which we were using as our H.L.S.

This was bad because of what had happened the past few week and we didn't have a H.L.S. Our A.O.R went to red so there was no flights in and we only had one day of water left.

After a few hours they decided to do a water drop for us and they dropped it in the flooded field "what a joke".

So we started to move the water into the PB (THAT WASN'T FUN). A few days past and the field dried up so we got choppered out and left six platoon there ("unlucky").

9th June

We got back to camp and once we got back we got told that in three hours we were going out on an op. Talk about a "shit buttie".

We moved out and headed towards the green zone when our platoon got told to push forwards and break right down the stream. Once we got to it our section commander told Monk to give it a good valon. So he started to search the stream and then he stepped on an I.E.D. I've heard the saying pink mist but you truly don't know what it means until you see it for yourself.

He ended up in the trees where he was searching. After I got myself up of the ground I just looked at him dangling from the branches, that's a site I'll never get out of my head.

I shouted over for another valon man to head towards him and clear the area so we could get him out of the tree.

After the stream had been cleared we got two lads to climb the tree and pass him down to us. At this time I had the OC shouting down the net about what's going on. All what I could say is wait out contact I.E.D, K.I.A and stay of the fucking net till I get back to you, out!

When we got him down I put him in a light weight stretcher and then my section commander said "what about his kit?" And I realized that his helmet weapon and legs weren't there so I sent out a 360 search for it all.

We found everything but one leg/boot so we made the decision to collapse an head back because of the time and the state of the lads. We headed back to camp and about one hundred meters up the hill on the way back I saw some black rubber in the shrubs. I told the front man to stop and valon up to it with me and that's when we found his other boot. So I picked it up and put it in my day sack being careful not to snap any bone.

When we got back to camp we took Monk to the aid station and handed him to the medics. We got told to go to the tents and get a shower because we were all covered with blood. I got to the shower and dropped my kit and then realised that I still had his leg. So I walked back to the aid point and give it to them. Whilst I was walking back I started to walk past the lads and they were just looking at me with their eyes wide open and I just said "forgot his leg" I just couldn't think of nothing else to say. So I dropped it off and got a shower.

16th June 05:30

We moved out of camp to go and enter compound 18 and 19 in the green zone. We moved through the green zone and entered the compound as a company.

We were in there for about ten minutes and then we came under fire by an unmarked compound and compound 5.

My section was on the roof and one and the rest of the section was around the sides of the compound. We got told by TAC to move out of the contact and head towards them. Whilst we were moving to their position (the local school) the contact got heavier.

The firing points were to the front and right and tac was on the high ground trying to give us some fire cover.

2 section moved back first and we crossed a bridge and went firm in a field. One section was meant to cross after us but they were pinned down. No one was moving so I shouted to my platoon sgt that I was going to go back and give them some fire power. He looked at me like I was insane and said "good idea yeah". So I pushed back over the bridge and started to engage the enemy from the hip(Rambo stile).

Once the enemy's head was down the pinned down section then moved through me.

Once all of them past me and we were in the field we started to fire monove back to tac's position. When we got to tac's position we then moved back to the fob.

19th June 2010

After the company's op we mounted Q.R.F. Nothing really happened, a few sangers had been contacted and we got mortared. They landed 100m from camp. A good bang though.

20th June 03:30

We moved out to the out skirts of Rahim and pushed into the green zone. Once we got to the top end of the village a few rounds were fired over our heads. We all went firm and looked for a firing point, nothing was seen.

After about ten minutes we moved out and pushed down from the high ground. We had two fields to cross which were open and there was a compound in the top left edge.

We pushed down and crossed a small stream and entered the first field and headed to a ditch which divided the two fields. We crossed over the ditch and headed into the field and towards the compound.

At this time the A&A was to our right and the tiger team was to our left in separate fields.

I was the last man of the section when I should have been the front man but my new section commander took no notice.

The section was about half way through the field when we got ambushed from the front. The ground next to me just exploded with rounds hitting it, the whole section dropped to the floor ("the shit hit the fan").

They were firing Dushkers, P.K.M's, and R.P.G's at us. After a lul in the battle I was shouting to the section commander has anyone been hit. He was shouting to the front man but he wasn't shouting back. Time was getting on at this point and no one was moving out of the field. So I hit the man in front of me to tell him to get in the ditch behind us and to pass it on. After a while the lads started to move back into the ditch and I started to move up to my section commander. Once I got to him I asked him "what the fuck he was doing, we've got to move back" and he replied "the front man isn't moving". So I told him that I was going to move up and give him front fire support so they can get back in the ditch.

I jumped up and a R.P.G flew past my head so I dropped back to the floor and leopard crawled past the lads. When I got to the front man I hit him on his leg and shouted "you hit" he didn't move. So I moved up to him and pulled him over whilst firing at the enemy. When I pulled him over he was fine not hit or nowt, he'd just froze. So I hit him on his helmet and told him to get in the fucking ditch.

He moved back and I started to fire at the compound in front of me, then called up to tac on the high ground to start firing so I can move back in the ditch.

Once tac was firing at the compound I turned around thinking that I would see a few of my section but I was on my own in the middle of the field (what a bunch of good lads!)

So I got up with rounds landing next to me and started to run for the ditch. When I was a few feet from it I jumped head first into it.

I looked at my section commander and said "where was you" he just looked and did a funny laugh and shrugged.

After a bit it died down and we moved out of the ditch and moved into a compound around the corner. We started to take some more incoming, that's when we called for air support. After they passed over it all died down.

In the afternoon there was a large explosion about 1km away and we got told that a local had set it off. We stayed in the compound that night and at first light we headed back to camp.

<u>23rd June 2010</u>

Not done much this past few days just been doing some admin. A chance to get my washing done and a bit of rest.

<u>Going on R&R</u>

I got a lift back to Bastion with the mail flight and stayed in Bastion 1 for a few days. On the second day when we were meant to fly back we got told that the flight had been delayed for twelve hours. When I heard this my head nearly exploded with anger, I've spent five months in this shit hole and I just want to go home and see my two girls. After I got calmed down we decided to go to the coffee house and chill out for a bit it's not like we didn't have time to kill.

The flight home took what seemed like for ages. We stopped off in Cyprus to refuel and then landed into Brize Norton. After six hours on the coach we eventually pulled into camp and that's when I saw Becky, what a beautiful site. I felt like dropping to my knees and bursting in tears but I kept it together and gave her the biggest hug. The smell of her perfume was the best smell ever. I don't know if it's because i've not smelt it for five month but god it smelt good!

Over my R&R I took Becky to the Hilton Tall Trees for a night which was good. It was good just to spend a bit of time with her.

After that I then visited the rest of my family. The look on my mum's face when I saw her was a picture. It was excitement and she looked so proud of me, which was a nice feeling.

After two short weeks at home I left for Afghan once again. The feeling of my heart sinking was horrible. I think it was a bit harder this time because I knew what I was going back to and how many near misses i'd had. I tried to keep it together and got back on the coach and headed back.

Back in Afghan

I've been back down Molvern once again "I thought i'd seen the last of that place" and we got stuck down there, you would of thought that they would had learnt by now.

There's so much stuff to write, so I won't bore you with most of it i'll just write the main parts.

I was on stage this time it was Sanger 1 next to the front gate. A patrol went out about ten in the morning and they were out for about two hours. I saw them coming back down the track so I started to give them some fire cover. The c/s was about half way back into camp when the floor just exploded from under them. Lads got thrown into the razor wire and into the river next to the camp. Luckily no one was hurt too much.

After the dust settled and we got the lads back in we realised that the Taliban had dug under the ground from a small out building next to the gate. We couldn't believe when we found this out so we got the go ahead to blow the out building up to prevent it happening once more.

The next day I just did my change over from Sanger 1 to Sanger 2. After a short time I heard an explosion in the dead ground in the front of the Sanger. About ten seconds later there was a dust cloud and then a man with a wheel barrow started to come down the track with a man lying in it. I told him to stop and aimed my weapon towards them he stopped and I called the medic up to me and a interpreter. The man told the turp that they found an I.E.D and he tried to move it. This just doesn't happen he was blatantly laying it. His hands and half of his face was missing. I asked the medic how long did he have till he would die and she said "probably three minutes, to bleed out." So I looked at my watch and timed three minutes then I let the medic go to help him.

"I nearly didn't put this part in but I thought if I'm going to write my true feelings and what I had experienced then I should put everything in".

This might be hard for some people to understand and I do get it but just take a moment and think of what they have done. So people might say you should of saved his life but all what I know is there is one less Taliban to blow me up!

Right or wrong you decide....

On the 23rd June we all got called to the centre of the camp this is where they always tell us bad news. They told us that three lads have been killed from C Company and they were Pte Isaac, Pte Dough and Lcpl David. There vehicle turned too sharply next to a river and it tipped into it, they couldn't get out and drowned late afternoon on the 22nd.

This was a big blow for C Company because they all were well respected. My thoughts go out to their families and friends they will be really missed and always remembered. God rest their souls.

On the 5th of July the company was starting a clearance op on the road which lead to Mulvern (PB line). This was the only road in and out for a resupply so the security of this road was paramount. The op started at 09:00 and within thirty minutes of the clearance Pte Sefton got blow up. He was crossing the dirt track and started to go down the away side bank when he stud on a pressure pan. He was hit to the front with all of the shrapnel and consequently he died. Pte Amera was hit to but Sefo took most of the blast. After they both got casi-vaced back to Bastion the op continued and they found 13 more I.E.D's. This road has now been re-named route Sefton.

I left Afghan by breaking my hand in six places. I wish I stayed there till the end but what happens happens I suppose and that's life....

Printed in the United States
By Bookmasters